BIG BOOK of RHYMES and STORIES

Chosen by Ronne Randall
Illustrated by Peter Stevenson

Contents
Nursery Rhymes

Nursery Tales
Traditional folk tales retold by Brian Morse

Animal Stories and Rhymes

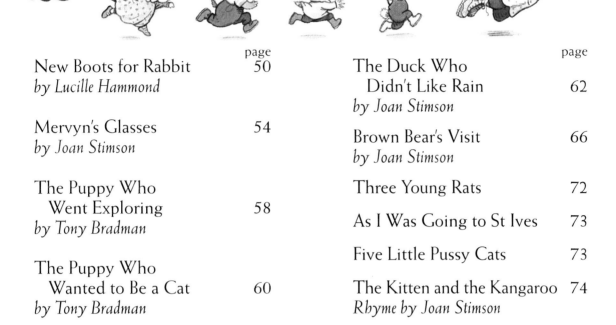

Bedtime Stories and Rhymes

Baa, Baa, Black Sheep

Baa, baa, black sheep, have you any wool?
Yes, sir, yes, sir, three bags full.
One for the master, and one for the dame,
And one for the little boy who lives in the lane.

Little Boy Blue

Little Boy Blue, come blow your horn!
The sheep's in the meadow, the cow's in the corn.
Where is the boy who looks after the sheep?
He's under the haycock, fast asleep.
Will you wake him? No, not I!
For if I do, he's sure to cry.

8

Mary Had a Little Lamb

Mary had a little lamb,
Its fleece was white as snow,
And everywhere that Mary went
The lamb was sure to go.

It followed her to school one day,
Which was against the rule.
It made the children laugh and play
To see a lamb at school.

And so the teacher turned it out,
But still it lingered near,
And waited patiently about
Till Mary did appear.

"What makes the lamb love Mary so?"
The eager children cry.
"Why, Mary loves the lamb, you know,"
The teacher did reply.

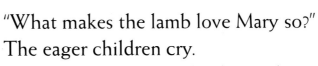

Goosey, Goosey, Gander

Goosey, goosey, gander,
　　Whither shall I wander?
Upstairs, downstairs,
　　In my lady's chamber.
There I met an old man
　　Who would not say his prayers.
I took him by the left leg
　　And threw him down the stairs.

Jack and Jill

Jack and Jill went up the hill
To fetch a pail of water.
Jack fell down and broke his crown,
And Jill came tumbling after.

Up Jack got, and home did trot,
As fast as he could caper,
To old Dame Dob, who patched his head
With vinegar and brown paper.

Humpty Dumpty

Humpty Dumpty sat on a wall,
Humpty Dumpty had a great fall.
    All the King's horses
    And all the King's men
Couldn't put Humpty together again.

Ride a Cockhorse

Ride a cockhorse to Banbury Cross,
To see a fine lady upon a white horse.
Rings on her fingers and bells on her toes,
And she shall have music wherever she goes.

Old King Cole

Old King Cole was a merry old soul,
And a merry old soul was he.
He called for his pipe, and he called for his bowl,
And he called for his fiddlers three.

Each fiddler he had a fiddle,
And the fiddles went tweedle-dee.
Oh, there's none so rare as can compare
With King Cole and his fiddlers three.

Sing a Song of Sixpence

Sing a song of sixpence,
A pocket full of rye.
Four and twenty blackbirds
Baked in a pie.

When the pie was opened,
The birds began to sing.
Wasn't that a dainty dish
To set before the King?

The King was in the counting house,
Counting out his money.
The Queen was in the parlour,
Eating bread and honey.

The maid was in the garden,
Hanging out the clothes,
When down came a blackbird
And pecked off her nose!

13

Hickory, Dickory, Dock

Hickory, dickory, dock,
The mouse ran up the clock.
The clock struck one,
The mouse ran down.
Hickory, dickory, dock!

Pussy Cat, Pussy Cat

Pussy cat, pussy cat, where have you been?
"I've been to London to visit the Queen."
Pussy cat, pussy cat, what did you there?
"I frightened a little mouse under the chair."

Grey Goose and Gander

Grey goose and gander,
    Waft your wings together,
And carry the good King's daughter
    Over the one-strand river.

I Had a Little Nut Tree

I had a little nut tree,
    Nothing would it bear
But a silver nutmeg
    And a golden pear.

The King of Spain's daughter
    Came to visit me,
And all for the sake
    Of my little nut tree.

The Old Woman Who Lived in a Shoe

There was an old woman who lived in a shoe,
She had so many children she didn't know what to do.
She gave them some broth without any bread,
Then scolded them soundly and sent them to bed.

I Saw a Ship A-Sailing

I saw a ship a-sailing,
    A-sailing on the sea,
And oh, but it was laden
    With pretty things for thee.

There were comfits in the cabin,
    And apples in the hold.
The sails were made of silk,
    And the masts were made of gold.

The four-and-twenty sailors
    That stood between the decks
Were four and twenty white mice
    With chains about their necks.

The captain was a duck
    With a packet on his back,
And when the ship began to move,
    The captain said, "Quack! Quack!"

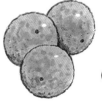

Oranges and Lemons

Oranges and lemons,
Say the bells of St Clement's.

You owe me five farthings,
Say the bells of St Martin's.

When will you pay me?
Say the bells of Old Bailey.

When I grow rich,
Say the bells at Shoreditch.

Pray, when will that be?
Say the bells of Stepney.

I'm sure I don't know,
Says the great bell at Bow.

Here comes a candle to light you to bed,
And here comes a chopper to chop off your head.

London Bridge

London Bridge is falling down,
    Falling down, falling down.
London Bridge is falling down,
    My fair lady.

Build it up with iron bars,
    Iron bars, iron bars.
Build it up with iron bars,
    My fair lady.

Iron bars will bend and break,
    Bend and break, bend and break.
Iron bars will bend and break,
    My fair lady.

Build it up with gold and silver,
    Gold and silver, gold and silver.
Build it up with gold and silver,
    My fair lady.

Gold and silver I've not got,
    I've not got, I've not got.
Gold and silver I've not got,
    My fair lady.

Then off to prison you must go,
    You must go, you must go.
Then off to prison you must go,
    My fair lady.

One, Two, Buckle My Shoe

One, two, buckle my shoe,

Three, four, knock at the door.

Five, six, pick up sticks,

Seven, eight, lay them straight.

Nine, ten, a big fat hen,

Eleven, twelve, dig and delve.

Thirteen, fourteen, maids a-courting,

Fifteen, sixteen, maids in the kitchen.

Seventeen, eighteen, maids in waiting,

Nineteen, twenty, my plate's empty.

To Market

To market, to market, to buy a fat pig,
Home again, home again, jiggety-jig.
To market, to market, to buy a fat hog,
Home again, home again, jiggety-jog.

This Little Pig

This little pig went to market,
This little pig stayed at home.
This little pig had roast beef,
This little pig had none.
And this little pig cried, "Wee-wee-wee,"
All the way home.

Little Bo-peep

Little Bo-peep has lost her sheep,
And doesn't know where to find them.
Leave them alone, and they'll come home,
Bringing their tails behind them.

Little Bo-peep fell fast asleep,
And dreamt she heard them bleating.
But when she awoke, she found it a joke,
For they were still a-fleeting.

Then up she took her little crook,
Determined for to find them.
She found them indeed, but it made her heart bleed,
For they'd left their tails behind them.

Jack Sprat

Jack Sprat could eat no fat,
His wife could eat no lean,
And so between them both,
They licked the platter clean.

Jack ate all the lean,
Joan ate all the fat.
The bone they picked clean,
Then gave it to the cat.

Old Mother Hubbard

Old Mother Hubbard
Went to the cupboard
To fetch her poor dog a bone.
But when she got there
The cupboard was bare,
And so the poor dog had none.

There Was an Old Woman

There was an old woman tossed up in a blanket,
    Seventeen times as high as the moon.
But where she was going no mortal could tell,
    For under her arm she carried a broom.
"Old woman, old woman, old woman," said I,
    "Whither, oh whither, oh whither so high?"
"To sweep the cobwebs from the sky,
    And I'll be with you by and by!"

Hey, Diddle, Diddle

Hey, diddle, diddle,
The cat and the fiddle,
The cow jumped over the moon.
The little dog laughed
To see such sport,
And the dish ran away with the spoon!

The Three Little Pigs

Once three little pigs decided it was about time they left home and found their own place to live. No sooner said than done. That very morning they packed up their things, kissed their mother goodbye, and set off.

They walked till midday. Then they sat by the road and ate half their sandwiches. After a nap they set off again. By suppertime the first little pig felt too tired to go any further.

"But we haven't got anywhere yet!" his brother and sister said. "What are you going to do for a house?"

They were next to a field full of wheat that had just been cut. "I'll build a house out of straw," the little pig said. He closed his eyes and went straight to sleep.

When the first little pig woke, the sun was sinking fast and the air was growing cold. And what was that dark hairy shadow in the wood? Suddenly he wished he'd gone on with the others. But he set to work, gathered together some straw, and built his house.

At midnight there came a tapping at his door. "Little pig, little pig, let me come in," a voice said. The little pig's blood ran cold. Now he knew what the shadow had been – a wolf!

"You're not coming in here, not by the hair on my chinny-chin-chin," he said in his most grown-up voice.

"Then I'll huff and I'll puff and I'll blow your house in!" the wolf snarled. "And that'll be the end of you." And it was.

Next morning the other pigs came back. What did they find? A heap of straw and all their brother's belongings torn up and scattered across the field. They ran away as quickly as they could.

By midday the two little pigs were exhausted and stopped running. The second little pig began to think that they had reached a very nice spot. There was a pile of wood that a woodcutter had left, perfect for building a big strong house.

"Whatever happened to my brother can never happen to me," thought the second little pig. But that night, as the church clock struck twelve, there came a tapping at her door.

"Little pig, little pig, let me come in," a voice said softly. "I'm lonely and hungry. I want a bite to eat."

The little pig's heart gave a thump. Now she knew what had happened to her brother. "Wolf! You don't fool me! You're not coming in, not by the hair on my chinny-chin-chin!" she cried.

"Then I'll huff and I'll puff and I'll blow your house in!" the wolf snarled. "And that'll be the end of you." And it was.

Next morning the third little pig found the wooden house shattered to pieces and all his sister's possessions blowing in the wind. He began to run away but then he thought, "What did my sister and I pass down the road yesterday? A brick factory!" Back he went and bought enough bricks to build a house.

That night the wolf came prowling and tapping again. "I'm a friend of your brother and sister," he called. "Little pig, little pig, let me come in."

"Wolf, you're not coming in here, not by the hair on my chinny-chin-chin!" the third little pig shouted.

"Then I'll huff and I'll puff and I'll blow your house in!" the wolf snarled. He drew a deep breath and huffed and puffed with all his might. A wind that would have torn up whole woods hit the house, but the walls stood firm because they were built of bricks. The wolf huffed and puffed again and again, but only the doors and windows rattled. In a towering rage, the wolf leapt up onto the roof and began to climb down the chimney.

But the third little pig had thought of this. He quickly built a roaring fire in the grate and put a huge pot of water on to boil. Instead of landing in the fireplace, the wolf fell into the pot and was boiled up. His skin popped open and out jumped the little pig's brother and sister! The wolf had gobbled them whole!

How happy the three little pigs were to see each other again! Safe and sound, in the house built of bricks, they lived happily ever after.

The Gingerbread Boy

Once upon a time an old lady thought how nice it would be to have a little boy about the house again.

"A boy?" her husband said. "We're too old for that sort of caper!" But he saw that she'd made up her mind so he said, "Why not bake a gingerbread boy?"

"What a marvellous idea!" the old lady exclaimed. She mixed up the ingredients, rolled out the dough, then cut out the shape of a gingerbread boy.

She gave him currants for eyes, a smiley mouth, a waistcoat and a hat. She even put buttons down the front of his waistcoat and go-faster stripes on his shoes! Then she popped him into the oven to bake.

When the timer on the cooker rang, the old lady opened the oven door. But the gingerbread boy didn't lie still on the baking tray. He leapt straight out onto the floor and ran away through the kitchen door. The astonished old man and lady called to him to come back, but the gingerbread boy felt very grown-up and he shouted,

"Run, run, as fast as you can,
You won't catch me, I'm the gingerbread man!"

Down the road he ran, through a stile and into a field where a cow was chewing grass.

"Hey!" the cow mooed. "Stop and give me a bite to eat!"

The gingerbread boy thought that was really funny. "I've run away from a man and a woman, and now I'll run away from you!" Putting on speed, he shouted,

> "Run, run, as fast as you can,
> You won't catch me, I'm the gingerbread man!"

The cow ran after him in a rather wobbly sort of way, but it was no use. She couldn't catch him.

Next the gingerbread boy came to a horse. "Hey!" the horse neighed. "I'm hungry. Give me a nibble!"

But the gingerbread boy just laughed. "I've run away from a man and a woman and a cow, and now I'll run away from you!" He ran even faster, shouting,

> "Run, run, as fast as you can,
> You won't catch me, I'm the gingerbread man!"

The horse galloped after him but he couldn't catch him.

Next the gingerbread boy met some joggers panting along a path. "Hey! Stop!" they called. "We haven't had our breakfast yet!"

But the gingerbread boy just skipped past them. "I've run away from a man and a woman and a cow and a horse, and now I'll run away from you!" Running even faster, he shouted,

"Run, run, as fast as you can,
You won't catch me, I'm the gingerbread man!"

The joggers ran as fast as they could after him, but there was no way they were ever going to catch him.

Then the gingerbread boy came to a river and there he had to stop. He could run but he couldn't swim.

There was a fox in the hedge who'd seen all that had gone on. He came strolling out. "Don't worry, sweet little gingerbread boy," he said. "I wouldn't dream of eating you. I've already eaten a hen and a turkey and some leftovers from a dustbin this morning. Do you want to cross the river?"

"Of course I do," the gingerbread boy said, looking over his shoulder at the man and the woman and the cow and the horse and the joggers, who were getting closer and closer.

"Then hop onto my tail," the fox said. "I'll swim you across." The gingerbread boy hopped onto the fox's tail and off they set, leaving all the gingerbread boy's pursuers behind.

When they'd gone a little way across the river, the fox said, "My tail's sinking into the water. You don't want to get wet, do you? Climb onto my back." The gingerbread boy did so.

They'd gone a little further when the fox said, "Now my body's beginning to sink too. Climb onto the tip of my nose. You'll be safer there. Gingerbread and water don't mix, do they?" The gingerbread boy climbed onto the tip of the fox's nose.

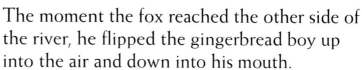

The moment the fox reached the other side of the river, he flipped the gingerbread boy up into the air and down into his mouth.

Snap! A quarter of him had gone.

Snap! A half of him had gone.

Snap! The fox ate the rest of him all in one go.

And that was the end of the gingerbread boy who'd been too fast for the man and the woman and the cow and the horse and the joggers, but not quick enough for the fox!

Goldilocks and the Three Bears

Once upon a time three bears lived in a house in the woods. They were called Tiny Little Bear, Middle-sized Bear and Great Big Bear. Their house, which they kept very spick and span, was full of just the right-sized things – bowls, cups, spoons, chairs, beds – anything you could think of.

One morning it was Great Big Bear's turn to get breakfast. He ladled the porridge into the bowls, just the right amount in each. But when they sat down to eat, the porridge was far too hot. The three bears decided to go for a walk while it cooled.

Two minutes after they had set off, who should come past their house but a little girl called Goldilocks. Goldilocks was a naughty spoiled little girl who always did exactly what she wanted. She shouldn't even have been in the woods (her mummy had sent her to the shop to buy some milk). But there she was and she knew the bears were out walking. She tried the door. It wasn't locked, so in she went.

34

Goldilocks spied what was on the table. "Porridge!" She licked her lips. "My favourite!" She tried the porridge in Great Big Bear's bowl first. "Ugh!" she said. "That's far too hot."

Next she tried Middle-sized Bear's bowl. "Ugh! That's far too cold!"

Last she tried Tiny Little Bear's. "Goody!" she said. "That's just right!" She gobbled it up. "Bother!" she said. "There wasn't much in there."

Then, because she needed a rest after all her wandering about in the woods, Goldilocks tried Great Big Bear's chair. "Hard as rocks," she said. "No good to me."

Next she sat in Middle-sized Bear's. "Miles too soft," she said.

Last she tried Tiny Little Bear's chair. "Just right," she said. At least she thought it was until her bottom went through the seat and the chair collapsed! "Bother!" she said again.

But Goldilocks was determined to get a rest. Upstairs she went and opened the bedroom door. First she tried Great Big Bear's bed, but that left her head too much in the air.

Next she tried Middle-sized Bear's. That left her feet too far up.

Last she tried Tiny Little Bear's. It was perfect! Without even taking off her shoes, she tucked herself in and went straight to sleep, dreaming of all the naughty things she'd get up to when she was older.

Meanwhile the bears returned home. They hung their coats up neatly and went to eat their porridge. Except, except…

"Who's been at my porridge?" Great Big Bear growled. "They've even left the spoon in it."

"And who's been at mine," asked Middle-sized Bear, "and done the same?"

"And who's been at mine, and eaten it all up?" Tiny Little Bear sobbed.

The three bears looked about. Someone had been in their house without permission and they didn't like that one bit.

"Somebody's been sitting in my chair," Great Big Bear growled, "and tossed my cushion on the floor!"

"Somebody's been sitting in my chair too," growled Middle-sized Bear. "My cushion's squashed."

"And somebody's been sitting in my chair and broken it," Tiny Little Bear said. He began to cry again.

"Sshh!" Great Big Bear said. "What's that noise?" The three bears listened.

"It's someone snoring," said Middle-sized Bear. The three bears looked at each other.

"They're still here!" Tiny Little Bear said. Upstairs they crept.

They went into the bedroom. "Somebody's been lying on my bed," Great Big Bear growled. "My cover's all creased."

"Somebody's been lying on my bed too," Middle-sized Bear grumbled. "The pillow's all out of place."

"And somebody's been lying *in* my bed, and they're *still* lying in it," squeaked Tiny Little Bear.

Great Big Bear's voice hadn't woken Goldilocks—she'd thought it was the wind roaring in her dream. Middle-sized Bear's voice hadn't woken her either—she'd thought it was her teacher shouting and that didn't frighten her at all. But Tiny Little Bear's shrill voice woke her straightaway.

She took one look at the bears standing in a row along one side of the bed, jumped out the other side and dived through the window. She landed in a bed of flowers only planted last week, knocked over the bird-table and ran straight out of the garden.

"She hasn't shut the gate," Middle-sized Bear complained with a sigh. "One of us will have to do it."

And what happened to Goldilocks no one knows. Maybe her mother just scolded her for not bringing the milk. Or maybe she did something worse, when she found out what Goldilocks had *really* been up to!

Little Red Riding Hood

Granny lived not far away, but to get to her cottage you had to walk through Bunny's Wood (though no one had seen a rabbit there for ages—you'll see why in a moment).

"Little Red Riding Hood!" her mother called. "Granny's still not very well. Put on your cloak and the pretty red riding hood she made for your birthday. Then pop over with this custard tart and pot of butter I've got ready for her tea."

So Little Red Riding Hood slipped on her cloak, fastened her riding hood under her chin, and set off.

"Remember to keep to the path in Bunny's Wood!" her mother called after her.

"Of course, Mummy," Little Red Riding Hood called back. "I always do."

She was only a little way inside the wood when there was a noise in the bushes and out onto the path jumped a great big wolf. Little Red Riding Hood nearly dropped her basket in fright, but actually the wolf seemed quite friendly. "Where are you off to, little girl?" he asked.

"To my granny's," Little Red Riding Hood replied. "It's the first cottage you come to at the end of Bunny's Wood. Granny's not very well. And my name's not 'little girl', it's Little Red Riding Hood."

"Sorry," said the wolf. "I didn't know. Tell you what – why don't I run ahead and tell Granny you're on your way? And, Little Red Riding Hood, don't stray off the path, will you? We don't want anything to happen to you before you get to Granny's, do we?"

Off skipped the wolf – just in time! For around the corner was a woodcutter. The wolf hadn't eaten Little Red Riding Hood there and then because he knew there was a woodcutter nearby who might come to her rescue.

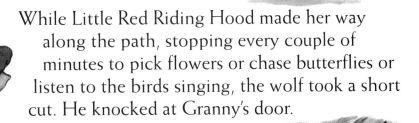

While Little Red Riding Hood made her way along the path, stopping every couple of minutes to pick flowers or chase butterflies or listen to the birds singing, the wolf took a short cut. He knocked at Granny's door.

"Who is it?" the little old lady called.

The wolf disguised his voice. "It's me, Little Red Riding Hood. I've brought some good things for tea."

"The door's on the latch, my darling," Granny called. And in went the wolf. How hungry he was! He hadn't eaten for days. He swallowed Granny whole, from her head to her feet.

About ten minutes later, Little Red Riding Hood knocked on Granny's door.

"Who is it?" the wolf called softly.

"It's me, Little Red Riding Hood."

"The door's on the latch, my darling," the wolf called. "Come on in."

For a moment Little Red Riding Hood hesitated. Wasn't there something funny about Granny's voice? Then she remembered that Granny had a cold. She lifted the latch and in she went.

The wolf was lying in bed wearing the little old lady's nightie and nightcap and glasses. The sheet was pulled right up over his face and he'd drawn the curtains to make it nice and dark.

"Put the things down there," he said, "then snuggle up to me, my darling."

Little Red Riding Hood put the custard tart and butter down on the bedside table but she didn't get onto the bed right away. Something suddenly struck her.

"What great big hairy arms you have, Granny!"

"All the better to hug you with, my darling!" the wolf said.

"And what great big ears you have, Granny!"

"All the better to hear you with, my darling!" the wolf said.

"And what great big eyes you have, Granny!"

"All the better to see you with, my darling!" the wolf said.

"And what great big teeth you have, Granny!"

"All the better to eat you with, my darling!"

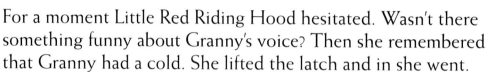

With that the wolf was so excited he couldn't contain himself any longer. He threw the bedclothes aside, jumped out of bed and swallowed Little Red Riding Hood whole, head first. Then he felt so happy and full of people that he lay back and went to sleep.

Unfortunately for the wolf, he was a loud snorer. A passing huntsman heard the snores. Thinking something was wrong with Granny, he crept into the cottage. He saw at once what had happened.

"I've been looking for you for months, you wicked creature," he cried, and he hit the wolf on the head with his axe handle. Then very carefully he slit the wolf's tummy open. Out popped Little Red Riding Hood and out popped Granny! They were completely unharmed.

Granny saw the custard tart and butter she'd been brought for her tea and, well, wolfed it down. Little Red Riding Hood promised Granny that she'd never be tricked by a wolf again. As she skipped home, she noticed that the rabbits had come out of hiding and Bunny's Wood was full of bunnies again.

"What a funny afternoon it's been," she thought.

The Three Billy Goats Gruff

Once there were three brothers, the three billy goats Gruff, who lived in a land of high mountains and deep ravines. One day the brothers were out chewing thorns and thistles on a stony hillside and not enjoying their food very much.

The smallest goat, whose mouth was much softer than his brothers', stopped for a rest. He looked over to the hillside opposite and what did he see? The most luscious green grass a billy goat had ever set eyes on!

"Brothers!" he bleated. "Follow me!" Down the bank he bounded. There was a stream at the bottom with a bridge over it, and the youngest billy goat began to run across the bridge.

"Stop!" his brothers shouted, but far too late. In the ravine under the bridge lived a troll with the sharpest teeth and ugliest eyes in the whole wide world.

"Stop! Stop!" the brothers called, but the troll was already poking his head over the edge of the bridge.

"Who's that trip-trapping over my bridge?" the troll screamed.

When he saw the troll, the smallest billy goat trembled from the tip of his wet nose to the end of his feathery tail.

"I'm little billy goat Gruff," he bleated. "I'm only crossing your bridge to get to the young green grass on the other side."

The troll licked his lips with his enormous rough tongue. "Oh no, you're not!" he shouted. He began to wriggle his way up onto the bridge. "I'm going to gobble you up."

"But my brother's coming after me!" the little billy goat bleated. "And he's much *much* fatter than me."

The greedy troll immediately dropped out of sight and the smallest billy goat ran on over the bridge to the other side.

The two older brothers put their heads together to decide what to do, and a minute later the middle-sized billy goat Gruff rather reluctantly came down the hillside. *Trip, trap, trip, trap,* went his hooves on the bridge. Immediately the troll raised his head above the edge.

"Who's that trip-trapping over my bridge?" he screamed.

"I'm middle-sized billy goat Gruff," the goat bleated, "and I'm going across to join my younger brother."

"Oh no, you're not!" the troll shouted. He began to clamber onto the bridge. "You look fat and juicy. I'm going to gobble you up."

"But my other brother's coming after me!" bleated the middle-sized goat, at the same time trying to make himself look as small as possible. "He's much, much, *much* fatter than me."

The greedy troll immediately dropped out of sight and, with a sigh of relief, the middle-sized billy goat ran over to the other side of the bridge.

After a minute the largest billy goat Gruff started trip-trapping over the bridge too. *Trip, trap, trip, trap, trip, trap,* went his hooves on the bridge.

The troll could hardly contain his excitement at the meal he was going to have. "Who's that trip-trapping over my bridge?" he screamed.

"I'm big billy goat Gruff," the third brother bleated, "and I'm going across to the other side to join my brothers in the lovely green grass."

"Oh no, you're not!" the troll shouted. "No, no, no!" With his long hairy arms he pulled himself straight up onto the bridge. "I'm going to gobble you up! That's what's going to happen!"

The moment the troll's feet landed on the bridge, he realized he'd made a big mistake. Big billy goat Gruff was massive. His horns were longer and sharper than all the troll's teeth put together.

As the goat put his head down and charged, the troll screamed, "No, no, no!" He tried to dive back under the bridge, but far too late. The goat's horns tossed him into the stream and the raging water carried him away. No one ever found out what happened to him and no one cared!

The big billy goat Gruff trip-trapped proudly over the rest of the bridge and joined his two brothers. Perhaps he had a few words to say to the smallest billy goat for putting them all in danger, but certainly the Gruffs enjoyed the young green grass and lived happily ever after.

Jack and the Beanstalk

There was once a poor widow. Her son Jack was a lazy boy, so they had very little money. One sad day things got so bad that the widow decided to sell the only thing they had left. She sent Jack off to market with Milky White, their cow, telling him to get the best price he could.

Jack was only part way along the road when he bumped into a funny old man. The old man eyed the cow and said, "My boy, I'll swap her for something very precious." He pulled five beans out of his pocket.

"Beans?" Jack said doubtfully.

"They're magic ones," the old man explained. That made Jack's mind up. He handed over Milky White and went home very satisfied with his bargain.

"Mum! Look what I've got!" he shouted. Jack's mother wasn't so happy, though. She threw the beans out of the window and a saucepan at Jack! Then she sent him to bed without any supper.

In the morning, however, Jack could hardly believe his eyes. Something was growing outside his bedroom window. He poked his head out. It wasn't a tree or a giant sunflower but a beanstalk that grew straight up into the sky. At once Jack clambered out of his window and began to climb the beanstalk.

46

Half an hour later he found himself in another country where everything was much larger. Across the fields was a very big house. A woman answered the door.

"What about a bite to eat?" Jack asked cheekily.

"All right," the woman said, "but if my husband the ogre comes, you'll have to make yourself scarce. He eats children."

Jack decided to take the chance, but he'd hardly sat down on the table when there was a roar outside.

"Fee-fi-fo-fum,
I smell the blood of an Englishman.
Be he alive or be he dead,
I'll grind his bones to make my bread."

"Quick! In the oven!" the woman said to Jack. "Nonsense, sweetheart, you can smell the scraps of yesterday's child I gave the cat," she shouted to her husband.

After his meal the ogre began counting bags of gold. That soon put him to sleep. Out sneaked Jack and stole a bag. He threw it down the beanstalk and scampered after. His mother could hardly believe their good luck.

But a few months later, all the gold spent, Jack decided to go back to the other land. Up the beanstalk he climbed. This time, however, the ogre's wife was more suspicious.

"Last time you came, a bag of gold went missing," she complained. "The fuss that caused!" All the same she let Jack in.

Very soon the ogre came along. *"Fee-fi-fo-fum,"* he started to roar. Jack hid in the oven again.

"Nonsense, angel," the ogre's wife said. "It's only the smell of that baby broth you had yesterday. Eat your buffalo pie."

After he'd eaten, the ogre shouted, "Wife, bring me my hen." His wife brought it. "Lay!" the ogre commanded, and to Jack's amazement the hen laid a golden egg. Naturally Jack stole the hen too.

By now Jack and his mother were well off, but after a year Jack decided to try his luck again. Up he climbed. This time he sneaked his way past the ogre's wife and hid in her copper pan.

In came the ogre. *"Fee-fi-fo-fum,"* he started.

"If it's that dratted boy again, he'll be in the oven, dearest," his wife said.

But of course Jack wasn't.

"I know he's here somewhere," the ogre rumbled, but although they searched high and low they couldn't find him.

This time after his meal the ogre got out a golden harp. "Sing!" he commanded, and the harp lullabyed him to sleep. Now Jack wanted that harp more than anything he'd ever wanted before. He climbed onto the snoring giant's knee, jumped onto the table and grabbed it.

"Master!" the harp cried. Jack jumped off the table. The ogre galloped after them. "Master!" the harp cried again, when Jack was halfway down the beanstalk. The ogre began to climb down after him.

"Mum!" Jack called. "Mum! An axe! Quick! Quick!" Together they chopped at the beanstalk and down it tumbled, ogre and all. He died instantly.

"Phew!" Jack said. "That was a close one!"

After that Jack and his mother lived rich people's lives. The hen laid golden eggs whenever they told it to. People paid to hear the golden harp play. It's even said that Jack married a beautiful princess. Maybe he did!

New Boots for Rabbit

One morning Rabbit looked outside and saw that it was raining. He remembered his new boots, and he hurried to put them on.

"It's raining out," said Rabbit to his mother. "Let's go for a walk so I can wear my new boots."

But Rabbit's mother was busy, and she said, "In a little while, Rabbit, when I finish my work."

So Rabbit began to play on his own, with his new boots on.

"With these boots," he whispered, "I could walk into a river and catch the biggest fish in the whole world." And he pretended he was a fisherman pulling in a huge fish.

Then Rabbit said to his mother, "Is it time to go for a walk now?"

"Later," replied his mother, because she was still busy.

So Rabbit played on his own some more.

"With these boots," he said, "I could be a sailor in a storm, travelling all over the world." And he pretended he was in a boat, tossing on the sea.

When he had finished playing, he called to his mother, "Are you ready yet?"

"Not quite," answered his mother.

One more time Rabbit went off to play.

"With these boots," he said, "I could be an explorer in the jungle." And he imagined himself walking through a rain forest, discovering birds and animals.

At last Rabbit heard his mother say, "Time to go now!" So, together, they went out for a walk.

But what a surprise! The rain had stopped, and the sun was drying up the puddles. Rabbit was so disappointed and cross that he felt like crying. He had waited all that time to get his new boots wet, and now the sun was shining!

Rabbit and his mother kept walking until they reached the park. Rabbit began to feel a bit better. He and his mother could look at the fountain with the little pool all around it, and that was always fun.

Suddenly someone shouted, "Oh, dear me, help!"

It was an elegant lady in smart clothes, and her hat had blown into the fountain.

"I'll get it!" said Rabbit, and quickly he waded into the little pool to rescue the hat.

"Oh, thank you," said the elegant lady when Rabbit returned the hat. "How lucky that you were wearing your boots." She smiled at Rabbit. "With boots like those, maybe someday you'll be a fisherman, or a sailor, or even an explorer!"

On the way home Rabbit felt very pleased and proud, and he skipped along in his new, wet boots. "With boots like these," he thought, "who knows *what* might happen?"

Mervyn's Glasses

It was dawn. Like all night birds, Mr and Mrs Owl were preparing for bed.

"I'm worried about Mervyn," said Mrs Owl. "I don't think he sees well."

"You worry too much, my dear," said Mr Owl, snuggling up to his wife. "Mervyn's just fine. Now you get a good day's sleep."

The Owl family slept all day. At dusk they woke up, and Mr Owl flew off to work.

All that night, Mrs Owl watched Mervyn carefully. She was right. Mervyn *couldn't* see well. He didn't always empty his plate. He held his new book too close to his eyes.

At bedtime Mrs Owl spoke to her husband again. "Tomorrow," she told him, "we must take Mervyn straight to Mr Specs. He'll soon put Mervyn right."

When Mervyn woke up, Mrs Owl explained the plan.

"But I don't want to wear glasses," said Mervyn. "They'll fall down my beak. They'll make me look silly."

"You'll look very handsome," Mrs Owl assured him. "Your father wears glasses, and there's nothing wrong with *his* looks!"

Mervyn enjoyed the visit to Mr Specs. Mr Specs tested his eyes with all kinds of charts and lenses. And Mervyn enjoyed choosing the frames for his glasses—it was fun seeing all the different shapes and colours they came in.

A week later, Mervyn and his mum went back to collect his glasses. Mr Specs held up a big mirror, and Mervyn saw himself clearly for the first time.

"What a fine bird I am!" he thought. "But I *don't* like my glasses!"

On the way home, Mervyn noticed all kinds of new things.

"Look at the stars!" he shouted. "And see those glow worms! These glasses work a treat."

But when he got home, Mervyn caught sight of himself in the mirror. "Silly old glasses!" he said to himself, stamping up and down his branch, crossly.

Just then the postman arrived. "Special delivery," he said, handing Mervyn a letter.

"What lovely big writing," said Mervyn. "It's an invitation," he told his parents, "to David's party. But I'm not going... *not in these glasses!*"

All week Mr and Mrs Owl tried to persuade Mervyn to change his mind. "Please go to the party," they said. "All your friends will be there. You don't want to disappoint David, do you?"

On the night of the party, Mervyn's dad tried one last time.

Mervyn shook his head.

"Well," said Dad, "if you don't want to play games and win prizes and eat a party tea, that's up to you. I only wish I could go!"

Mervyn started to think about all the other owls having fun. He thought about the sandwiches and lemonade and cake and ice cream. And in the end he decided to go to the party. He wrapped David's present and brushed his feathers. Then he flew there, all by himself.

David was waiting on his branch to greet Mervyn.

Mervyn landed gracefully and held out the present. And when he looked up at David, he got a super surprise.

David was wearing glasses, too. And he looked *so* handsome!

The Puppy
Who Went Exploring

Prudence the puppy was very excited. It had been such a thrilling day! She had started it living in one place, and now she was living somewhere completely different.

Her family had moved into a new house. Prudence couldn't wait to go exploring, even though she'd be going on her own. Her mum and dad and sister all said they had too much to do.

"See you later, everybody," she said, and trotted off.

"Don't get into any mischief, now," her dad called.

"Really," thought Prudence, "as if I would!"

Prudence went through the nearest door, and found herself approaching a cave full of interesting things. She snuffled inside it for a while, but then the things attacked her.

"Yikes!" said Prudence. "I'm off!"

She skidded into a nearby room, where she saw a strange box thing standing in the corner. She stood on her hind legs and sniffed at it... and suddenly it made a very loud noise!

"Yikes!" said Prudence. "I'm off!"

She scampered up the stairs and dashed into another room. There she found a big, puffy thing that was just right for biting and tugging... but it tried to smother her!

"Yikes!" said Prudence. "I'm off!"

She shot across the landing, rolled down the stairs, and landed at the bottom with a *bump*! And that's where the rest of the family found her when they came running.

"Prudence!" said her mum. "What *do* you think you're up to?"

"Quick, everybody," said Prudence breathlessly. "Let's get out of here before it's too late…"

When they'd stopped laughing, Prudence's family showed her round the house. She discovered that the cave was a broom cupboard, the box thing was a television, and the puffy thing a duvet. To make her feel more cheerful, Prudence's dad found her a bone. And next time she went exploring – she didn't go alone!

The Puppy
Who Wanted to Be a Cat

Life seemed far too busy for Penny the puppy. There was always something her parents wanted her to do, and she was fed up with it. So one day, Penny decided to be… a cat.

"Cats can do whatever they like," Penny said to her brother and sister. "I mean, just look at Ginger!"

Penny and her family shared the house with Ginger the cat. He did an awful lot of dozing and was never, ever, in a hurry.

"But you're a dog," said Penny's brother. "You can't be a cat."

"Oh, can't I?" said Penny. "We'll soon see about that!"

From then on, Penny copied everything Ginger did. She walked like a cat, stretched out on the rug like a cat, and even tried to miaow like a cat, although that was quite hard.

And when her parents told her to do something, she said, "I'm sorry, I can't do that. I'm a cat!"

As you can imagine, after a while this started to drive her parents *crazy*. So they came up with a plan…

The next morning there was a surprise for Penny. At breakfast, her brother's bowl was full of lovely, chunky dog food, and so was her sister's. But Penny's contained something rather strange.

"What's *this?*" asked Penny, sniffing at it.

"Well, since you're a cat now," said her mother, "we thought you ought to have cat food for your meals!"

Suddenly Penny wasn't so sure being a cat was such a good idea. How could Ginger eat this disgusting stuff? It was so *yucky*…

The rest of the family burst out laughing at the look on Penny's face. Penny laughed too when her father took away the bowl of cat food and produced a proper breakfast for her.

And from then on Penny was a puppy again. At least she was — until she saw a bird flying through the sky.

"Don't be absurd," said her sister. "You can't be a bird!"

But Penny's parents wouldn't put anything past her.

And neither would I!

The Duck
Who Didn't Like Rain

Derek was a new duckling. He lived with his family by the Big Pond.

Mr and Mrs Duck were proud of their ducklings. Every morning they took them for a long walk.

It was a long, dry spring that year. But at last it rained. And that's when the trouble started.

Mrs Duck was excited to see the rain. She lifted her wing carefully and woke the ducklings. "Look, children," she said. "It's a lovely wet day!"

The ducklings rubbed the sleep from their eyes. "Is that the rain you told us about, Mum?" they asked, beeping with excitement.

"Yes, indeed," she said. "Now hurry and line up. Your father's ready to go!"

"Let us proceed!" cried Mr Duck, and the Duck family set off in a long line. But Derek lagged behind.

"What is it, dear?" asked his mother gently.

"Don't like it," said Derek in a small voice. "Don't like the rain. Makes my toes feel tickly."

"Makes your *toes* feel tickly?" cried Derek's father. "Whoever heard of a duckling with tickly toes?"

Mrs Duck didn't shout. That evening she paid a visit to Old Ma Goat. Ma Goat kept a shop, and she sold almost everything you could think of.

Mrs Duck was in luck. Ma Goat had some wellingtons, just the right size for Derek.

Next time it rained, Mrs Duck gave Derek the wellingtons.

"Let us depart!" cried Mr Duck.

"How's that, Derek?" asked Mrs Duck gently.

"Still don't like it," whispered Derek. "Musses up my feathers. Spoils my hair."

"Spoils your *hair?*" cried Derek's father. He was very upset to have a child who worried about his hair.

63

Mrs Duck went back to Old Ma Goat. What luck! Ma Goat had a smart cape and hood, just the right size for Derek.

Next time it rained, the Duck family shouted cheerfully, "Hurry up, Derek. Put on your cape and wellingtons."

"How's that, dear?" asked Mrs Duck.

"It's *lovely*, Mum," replied Derek.

Suddenly he saw a huge rainbow. "What's *that*?" he asked.

"That, my boy," said his father, "is a rainbow. A rainbow comes when the sun tries to shine through the rain."

"It's beautiful!" said Derek, gazing up at the bright colours. Then he looked around in wonder. Everything sparkled in the rain!

After that, Derek wanted it to rain every day. He didn't always see a rainbow. But he loved exploring in the rain. And sometimes he was in such a hurry to get started that he even forgot to put on his cape and wellingtons!

Brown Bear's Visit

Brown Bear had just finished breakfast. "That was horrible," he grumbled. "What's next?"

"Next," said Mum, "you can go to the playground while I tidy up."

At the playground, Brown Bear began to grizzle. "Same old friends, same old slide. It wouldn't be so bad if we had a climbing frame here!"

Brown Bear was grouchy all day. Then, when he got home, Mum sent him off to the waterfall for a shower.

"I hate getting clean!" he moaned. "Why can't I stay dirty sometimes?"

Brown Bear grumbled as he gobbled his supper. He grizzled as he snuggled into bed. Mum tucked him in and told him a story.

"That was boring," he yawned. Then he turned over and fell asleep.

Next morning Brown Bear had a visitor. It was his cousin Billy Bear from across the mountain.

"Can you come to play?" Billy Bear asked. "Mum says you can stay the night."

Brown Bear was so keen to go he barely said goodbye to his mum. He didn't even wave to his friends on the slide. He just jogged along beside his cousin and asked what they were going to do first.

"First," said Billy Bear, "we'll go to the playground so I can show you our climbing frame. Then I'll take you home to meet the twins."

Brown Bear couldn't wait to try the climbing frame. "It's easy," said Billy. "Just watch me and my friends!" And they clambered up to the top of the climbing frame and began swinging from the highest bars.

Brown Bear tried to do the same. But he had never climbed so high before. He fell off and bumped his nose!

Billy didn't seem to notice. He carried on climbing and swinging with his friends until it was time to go home.

As they neared home, Brown Bear smelt something cooking. The thought of food cheered him up. But Auntie was behind schedule.

"It's those twins," she explained. "They're always under my feet!"

But then she had a brainwave. "Why don't you big bears take the little ones to the river? You can bath them for me. And bath yourselves at the same time."

"I don't like rivers," said Brown Bear. "Why can't we go to the waterfall?"

"Because we don't have one," said Auntie simply, as she began to tidy up.

As soon as they reached the river, the twins squirted Brown Bear and Billy. Then, just when it was time to go home, they rolled on the bank and got all dirty again – and splashed mud all over Brown Bear and Billy. Brown Bear had *never* been so cross – or so hungry!

"Here you are at last," said Auntie, when they finally got home. But as soon as she brought in supper, the other bears swooped down like vultures. There was hardly anything at all left for Brown Bear.

Brown Bear's tummy was still rumbling when he went to bed. It was so dark he couldn't even see his cousins.

"Can I have a story?" he called out.

But Auntie was already snoring. And so were all the other bears.

The next day Billy led Brown Bear along the track. He pointed in the direction of Brown Bear's home. "Look," he said. "Your mum's coming to meet you."

Brown Bear barely said goodbye to his cousin. He bounded along the track as fast as his legs would carry him.

"It *is* good to see you, Brown Bear," said Mum. "Now, what would you like to do first?"

Brown Bear nestled up to Mum. He put his nose in the air and breathed in the sweet smells of home.

"Lovely friends! Lovely slide! Lovely waterfall! Lovely meals! Lovely stories!" he cried. "And I want to do it *all* first!"

Three Young Rats

Three young rats with black felt hats,
Three young ducks with new straw flats,
Three young dogs with curling tails,
Three young cats with demi veils,
Went out to walk with two young pigs
In satin vests and sorrel wigs.
But suddenly it chanced to rain,
And so they all went home again.

As I Was Going to St Ives

As I was going to St Ives,
I met a man with seven wives.
Each wife had seven sacks,
Each sack had seven cats,
Each cat had seven kits.
Kits, cats, sacks, wives,
How many were going to St Ives?

(Answer: Only one — "I".)

Five Little Pussy Cats

Five little pussy cats sitting in a row,
Blue ribbons round each neck, fastened in a bow.
Hey, pussies! Ho, pussies! Are your faces clean?
Don't you know you're sitting there so as to be seen?

The Kitten
and the Kangaroo

The kitten and the kangaroo
Were bored and wondered what to do.
"I know," said Kanga, "take a ride!
Here's my pouch – just hop inside."

The kitten took a mighty leap.
"I say," she said, "you're mighty steep!"
"Come on," said Kanga, "grab a paw,
I'll take you on a guided tour."

The twosome bounced across the town.
"Gee-up!" said Kitten. "Don't slow down!"
But Kanga groaned, "I've had enough.
I'm high on bounce and low on puff."

"But I've no pouch," the kitten cried,
"To give my weary friend a ride."
She thought and sighed and thought some more,
Then rushed off to the superstore.

The boss was kind. He heard her plan.
"I'd like to help you if I can.
Here's a trolley – take good care –
I think your friend could fit in there."

So Kanga rode back home in style,
While Kitten pushed and gave a smile.
"I may be small, but you will find
I'll *never* leave a friend behind!"

The Bear and the Babysitter

The new babysitter was due any minute. And Buster was sulking in Ben's room.

The last babysitter had been bossy and banished them to bed early. The babysitter before that had been fussy. *She'd* scrubbed behind their ears!

And now… *ding, dong!*

Help! Here she is! thought Buster. And he slid smartly into Ben's playhouse.

Buster could hear hello and goodbye noises coming from the hall. Then he heard Ben calling his name.

But, although Buster sat in the playhouse for a long time, there were no getting-ready-for-bed noises. And once or twice he thought he heard squeaks of excitement.

Buster padded softly onto the landing and listened again.

"Oh no!" he groaned. "They're playing my favourite game. And they've started without me!"

Buster squirmed with disappointment.

Then — *Brring! Brring!* — the phone rang in the kitchen.

Whoosh! As soon as the babysitter left the living room, Buster whizzed down the stairs.

"A wrong number," the babysitter explained, coming back into the hall. Then she caught sight of Buster at the bottom of the stairs, looking innocent and interesting.

"Look, Ben!" she cried. "I told you your teddy would turn up. Now he can join in our game."

Buster and Ben went to bed late that evening. There was barely time to wash before their story. And, when she tucked them in, the babysitter smiled kindly.

"The first family I babysat for," she confided, "were a bit bossy. And the next family were fairly fussy. But this must be third time lucky," she said, "because you two are *brilliant!*"

And so are you, thought Buster. *And so are you.*

Midnight in the Park

You know the bear from Number Nine,
She likes to play at night.
Down the drainpipe watch her whizz,
There's not a soul in sight.

She tries a cartwheel on the grass,
She longs to stretch her paws.
Then on the swing she starts to sing,
"It's great to be outdoors!"

"Psst!" Someone's creeping up the path,
They want to try the slide.
It's Twenty-three and Seven B:
"We couldn't stay inside!"

Now Twenty-two is coming too,
And Seventeen and Four,
They're jumping off the climbing frame,
Then running back for more.

But suddenly a light appears,
"What's going on out there?"
A small boy cries and tries to see,
"And where's my teddy bear?"

Up the drainpipe, home they go,
Before it starts to rain,
They leave the park all still and dark,
But they'll be back again!

Scaredy Kitten

On the night before Christmas, Prescott was all bundled up, ready to go carol singing with his sister Sylvia and their friends. He opened the front door and peered outside.

"Gosh!" he thought. "It's dark. Very dark."

"It's too cold for me," Prescott said to Sylvia.

"It is not," Sylvia said. "You're just afraid of the dark. What a scaredy kitten!"

Prescott went to his room and took off his scarf and hat and mittens and boots. He put on his pyjamas, turned on his night light and crawled into bed.

"Oh no!" he said suddenly. "How could I forget?"

He got out of bed and pulled the window blind down tight. Then he drew the curtains, to make sure he couldn't see the night.

Prescott *was* afraid of the dark. He couldn't tell where the darkness ended and everything else began. He felt as if he were disappearing in the dark. And that made him very nervous.

Most of the time it didn't matter that Prescott was afraid of the dark. But sometimes it mattered a lot.

On Halloween, Prescott got into his ghost costume, ready for trick-or-treating. He thought that maybe the bright white sheet would help keep him from disappearing in the dark.

But when he stepped outside, he saw that it was rainy and foggy, and *very* dark. *Everything* had disappeared!

"It's too wet for me," said Prescott, going back inside.

"Scaredy kitten!" said Sylvia.

Prescott stayed indoors that night and greeted the other trick-or-treaters at the door. They were all smiling or laughing. Prescott hid his sad face behind his mask.

Just a few days later it was Bonfire Night. Everyone was going to the village green to watch the fireworks. Everyone except Prescott.

"I'm too sleepy," said Prescott, pretending to yawn. "Maybe I'll watch from my bedroom window."

"Scaredy kitten!" said Sylvia.

Prescott went up to his room and tried to watch the fireworks from the window. But he ended up turning on his night light, pulling the blind down and drawing the curtains to keep out the night. He never saw any fireworks at all.

A few weeks later it was Prescott's birthday. His grandpa came to his party and brought a special present. When Prescott opened the box, he didn't know what it was.

"This is a telescope," Grandpa explained. "You take it outside at night and look through it to see the sky up close. You'll be surprised when you see what's up there. But we have to wait until it's dark."

Prescott didn't want to be surprised in the dark. He didn't want to go outside at night at all.

"Scaredy kitten," whispered Sylvia. "I bet you don't go!"

But Prescott loved Grandpa very much, and he couldn't disappoint him. So when it got dark, he went outside with Grandpa and the telescope. He held Grandpa's hand very tightly.

Grandpa showed Prescott how to hold the telescope up to his eye and look up at the sky. "Just look through it and tell me what you see," he said to Prescott.

Prescott looked.

"I see stars," he said. "Oh! Look at them! They're so shiny! And look at the moon! The moon is so bright! It's like a huge torch! Wow!"

Prescott was amazed. And when he took the telescope away from his eye, the night didn't seem so dark any more.

"Is the moon there every night?" he asked.

"Yes," replied Grandpa. "On cloudy or foggy nights you can't see the moon or the stars, but they're always there. You can count on them!"

"I can?" Prescott asked.

Grandpa smiled. "Yes," he said. "I knew you'd be surprised. I'll bet you didn't know there was so much light in the night."

When Prescott went to bed that night, he didn't turn on his night light or pull down his window blind or draw the curtains. The stars shone in the window and the moon gleamed brightly.

Prescott smiled as he watched the light of the night glowing in his room. He wasn't afraid of the dark any more.

The Elves and the Shoemaker

There was once a shoemaker who was very poor although he was a master craftsman. Every day he seemed to get even poorer. In the end he sold so few shoes that he had no money to buy leather to make new ones. At last he only had one piece of leather left.

That night he cut out the leather and, with a sigh, left it on his workbench ready to stitch up into his last pair of shoes in the morning. As he went upstairs to bed, he could only think that if a miracle didn't happen he would have to sell his shop.

The next morning, when he opened his workroom door, the shoemaker saw something extraordinary. On his bench stood the most beautifully made pair of shoes he'd ever seen. He darted to pick them up. He turned them round in his hands. He couldn't have made them better himself!

That morning a rich man walked past the shop. He saw the pair of shoes in the window and liked them so much that he was willing to pay twice what the shoemaker asked!

Now the shoemaker had enough money to buy leather for two more pairs of shoes. That evening he cut them out and left them on his workbench. In the morning, to his great joy, the leather had been stitched up into *two* beautiful pairs of shoes. The shoemaker was able to sell them for enough money to buy leather for *four* pairs of shoes.

For some time, things went on like this. Soon the shoemaker's little shop became so famous that rich ladies and gentlemen from all over the country came to see what he had to sell.

But one day towards Christmas, the shoemaker, who was a kind-hearted man, said to his wife, "Don't you think we ought to see who's doing us this favour? Think how poor we once were and how well off we are now. Tonight let's stay downstairs with the light off and see who comes." So instead of going to bed, the shoemaker and his wife hid behind the workroom door. As quiet as mice they waited.

As midnight struck from the tower of the parish church, the shoemaker's wife nudged her husband. Two tiny elves, dressed in rags, were clambering up onto the workbench. They ran around looking at what work they had to do. Then they seized the shoemaker's tools and began. As they worked they sang,

> "Stitch the, stitch the, stitch the shoes,
> Fit for kings and queens to choose!
> Dart the needle, pull the stitch.
> Work, work, work, to make the cobbler rich!"

Long before dawn they'd finished their work and slipped away.

The shoemaker and his wife got up late next morning. Over breakfast the wife said, "Think how cold those poor little creatures must have been! Their feet were bare and their clothes were just rags. It made me shiver just to look at them. Don't you think we ought to make them a present to say 'thank you' for all the work they've done for us?"

The shoemaker agreed, and he and his wife set to work immediately. That night they left the tiniest clothes and shoes you could imagine on the workbench.

At midnight, as the church clock struck, the elves appeared again. At first they seemed puzzled to find no shoes to stitch, but suddenly they realized what kind of presents had been left for them. With whoops of joy they pulled on the tiny clothes and shoes. Then they began to dance all around the room, leaping on and off the table, balancing along the backs of the chairs, and swinging off the curtains. As they played they sang,

"The shoemaker has no more need of elves.
Now let him stock his own shelves!"

With that they ran out of the door and across the churchyard. They never came back. The shoemaker was sad to see them go but he could hardly complain after all the work they'd done for him. And they seemed to leave a little of their magic behind them, for he and his wife were lucky for the rest of their lives.

Twinkle, Twinkle

Twinkle, twinkle, little star,
How I wonder what you are!
Up above the world so high,
Like a diamond in the sky.

When the blazing sun is gone,
When he nothing shines upon,
Then you show your little light,
Twinkle, twinkle, all the night.

In the dark blue sky you keep,
And often through my curtains peep,
For you never shut your eye,
Till the sun is in the sky.

Jane Taylor

Star Light

Star light, star bright,
First star I see tonight,
I wish I may, I wish I might,
Have the wish I wish tonight.

Good Night

Good night,
Sleep tight,
Wake up bright
In the morning light
To do what's right
With all your might.